BAD Nana

OLDER NOT WiSeR

Olivia

for all the Nanas — stay bad

First published in Great Britain by
HarperCollins *Children's Books* in 2018
Published in this edition in 2019
HarperCollins *Children's Books* is a division of HarperCollins*Publishers* Ltd,
HarperCollins Publishers
1 London Bridge Street
London SE1 9GF

The HarperCollins website address is:
www.harpercollins.co.uk

4

Text and illustrations copyright © Sophy Henn 2019
All rights reserved.

ISBN 978–0–00–826806–0

Sophy Henn asserts the moral right to be identified
as the author and illustrator of the work.

Typeset in New Clarendon 14/22pt by Goldy Broad
Printed and bound in China by RRD Asia Print Solutions

MIX
Paper from
responsible sources
FSC
www.fsc.org
FSC™ C007454

This book is produced from independently certified FSC™ paper
to ensure responsible forest management.

For more information visit: www.harpercollins.co.uk/green

BAD Nana

OLdeR NoT WiSeR

Sophy Henn

HarperCollins *Children's Books*

CONTENTS

SUPER DUPER

STAY WEIRD

IT'S NICE TO BE NICE

Drama Rama

Future PM

SMILE

SUPER DUPER

YAY

You got this, Kiddo! xxx

BAD Nana

B TEAM

SMILE A WHILE

What are you staring at?

THiNGS YOU SHOULD kNOW

OLLY GOOD ALL ROUNDER

One is called *Granny Rose* and she is very nearly completely **peach-coloured**. Even her hair. She smells like talc and flowers, and everything in her house has a tiny **lace mat** underneath it. Cups, vases, china lambs,

plates, bowls of fruits,

EVERYTHING . . .

19

Except for the
toilet roll –
that has
a dress.

I am not even joking.

My other grandma is called

BAD NANA.

Well, that's not her actual, actual name. I can't even remember what that is as we only ever call her BAD NANA and she doesn't even mind. In fact, I think she quite likes it.

BAD NANA is very different from Granny Rose and Shirley. Her face is quite a lot more pointy and her glasses are enormous. She has jet-black hair that comes out of a bottle, but I haven't a clue how. She wears a BLACK dress, pointy BLACK shoes and gigantic earrings. She says they are for a little bit of twinkle . . .

but I have **no idea** what
that **actually** means.

For someone on the small side, **BAD NANA** has a completely ginormous handbag.

She's never EVER without it. It is black and shiny and smells like new shoes. I actually haven't properly seen inside it – I don't think anyone has – apart from **BAD NANA**. But based on guesswork and memory this is what I think is in there . . .

For back-up or **extra-long** journeys or just shopping she has her even more **humongous** tartan trolley. What's inside that is quite a **mystery** and if I'm a hundred per cent truthful I am NOT at all sure I even **want** to know. She also has a walking stick with her at **all** times.

No one is completely sure if BAD NANA actually NEEDS the stick for walking purposes. But we definitely DO know she needs it for tapping TALL people on the shoulder, *reaching* high-up shelves in the supermarket, tripping people up and waggling it about when she is cross.

On super-special occasions **BAD NANA** pops on her SPARKLY pink turban. I am not exactly sure why – maybe you need MORE twinkle for special occasions . . . I really don't know as I find I don't really need any twinkle EVER.

But **BAD NANA** says it gives her an air of mystery. Well, if the mystery is WHERE IS THE ALIEN OVERLORD HIDING? then she's SPOT on!

BAD NANA lives at 66 Broadbottom Road, which is exactly eight minutes and thirty-six seconds from my house, if you get a wiggle on. Or five years if you are Jack and take FOREVER to walk ANYWHERE. He really has NO sense of urgency.

Her house looks a bit like a **toadstool** because it's mainly **roof** and not so much **house**. This seems to be how OLD people like their houses as there are practically hundreds around and about where **BAD NANA** lives and they **all** have OLD people living in them.

I actually do like **BAD NANA'S** house,
though, because you **never** need to
wear a jumper, there are **always** biscuits
and it **smells** of tea and mischief. It's a
good job I DO like it, because I am round
at **BAD NANA'S** house A LOT. My mum works
and my dad does too, so they are always
busy right up to their **eyeballs**. I am
mainly there after school, but sometimes
before and sometimes **even** on Saturdays.
But NOT Sundays, for Pete's sake.

Unfortunately Jack has to be at **BAD NANA'S** A LOT too, which is very annoying as he ruins everything. I am certain **BAD NANA** feels the same way I do about Jack and wishes he had never been born, but she is very good at hiding it and won't ever admit it, even though I ask her all the time and promise NOT to tell Jack. Which is extremely kind of her when you think about it.

Liberace the cat lives at **BAD NANA'S** house too. Liberace is NOT like any other cat I have ever seen. There are two main reasons for this.

The first is that Liberace is pink. I am almost ninety-eight per cent certain this is **BAD NANA'S** doing as cats are usually ginger or black or white, or black AND white, but almost NEVER pink. **BAD NANA** swears Liberace is completely *entirely* naturally pink, but I strongly feel this is not *quite* the truth as Wilf pinkie-promised he saw Liberace under one of the dryers at *Silveen's Salon* in town. And that's where you go if you want pink or lilac or even mint-green hair.

The other main reason *Liberace* is unusual is because he looks surprised about EVERYTHING. From the moment he opens his eyes he looks like he is being surprised again and again and AGAIN, like he is never NOT being surprised.

Personally I like surprises, but *Liberace* doesn't look like he enjoys them at all. Which is a shame, seeing as he seems to have more surprises than anyone I know.

The many faces of Liberace

Happy

Sad

Furious

Silly

People are **always** popping in at **BAD NANA'S** and the person that pops in the **most** is **BAD NANA'S** very **best** friend, Cynth. She just lives over the road so it's really handy. They giggle A LOT and although I don't **always** understand what they are giggling about I am **very** happy that they do. It's **nice** to know you can still have **fun** with your best friends **even** when you are really

really really

really really

OLD.

Someone who definitely NEVER pops round to **BAD NANA'S** is Mrs Farquar-Haha. Her name would suggest she is lots of fun, but actually she is the opposite of fun. This is probably why she and **BAD NANA** NEVER agree on anything.

Mrs Farquar-Haha is very important in ALL the things that happen where we live. She's ALWAYS at every event with a clipboard, looking down her nose at EVERYTHING. I don't really know what started the feud between Mrs Farquar-Haha and **BAD NANA**, but it pops up every now and again, like when **BAD NANA** snuck diarrhoea tablets in Mrs Farquar-Haha's trolley at the shops and got Beryl to price-check them on the tannoy.

41

Or when Mrs Farquar-Haha BANNED
BAD NANA from the line-dancing club
for being disruptive in the
freestyle section.

We thought they might have made friends when they were ACCIDENTALLY locked in the village hall the night before the summer fair and ate all the liqueur chocolates from the tombola stand to survive (it was *only* two hours).

Anyway, by the time the caretaker got them out they were looking a bit the worse for wear and doing a two-person conga around the hall. But instead of ending the feud it only seemed to make it WORSE.

And it seems the feud has been passed down to me because Georgina Farquar-Haha (Mrs Farquar-Haha's granddaughter) is a total MEANIE and makes my life really rotten at every chance she gets. Sometimes I feel like I am tiptoeing on eggshells so I don't do anything embarrassing or silly or funny for her to TEASE me about until the end of time.

Wilf and Marcy,
and *even* Sukey,
say I shouldn't
worry about her
and I really try
NOT to, but when
someone gets the whole
class to call you Eggy
for a WHOLE term for
having egg sandwiches
ONCE (thanks, Dad) then I
really think you can't be **too careful**.

And, yes, she is **rubbish** at thinking
up **nicknames**.

I honestly don't know how
she gets away with it.

And I also honestly don't know where
BAD NANA got her name from.

I mean she's
not bad...

or bad . . . .

. . . or even BAD.

She's more up-to-no-good.

Or completely EMBARRASSING.

Or a little bit cheeky.

But she's nearly always GOOD
FUN. Things always seem to happen
when BAD NANA'S around. You never know
what's next.

It can be exciting and very often ends
in BIG TROUBLE, but usually for
BAD NANA because Dad says she should
know better.

But I'm very glad she doesn't.

NO FUN

PARKIE

catch a falling leaf and get 1 WISH

GR8

I scream for ICE CREAM

BAD
Nana

THE
BEE'S
KNEES

PArk
LiFe

I ♥
BOOKS

POW

WEAR
BADGES

If the sun has got his hat on, **BAD NANA** is **always** taking us to the **park**. I think this is because it is **free** and isn't the television.

BAD NANA always goes straight to "**her**" bench as she says her sitting-on-the-grass days are **long** gone. She can't remember sitting on the floor at all after the millennium, but I don't think the two things are even **slightly** linked.

The Park

Sometimes someone else is sitting on "her" bench, but this isn't a problem as BAD NANA just walks over, points to the plaque on the bench that says *In loving memory of Bill* and wobbles her bottom lip until whoever is sitting there moves. Sometimes she makes me and Jack stand behind her and look sad, just to be sure.

I asked **BAD NANA** if she actually knew *Bill*. She just said that wasn't the point, and anyhow she always gave *Bill*'s plaque a quick polish with her spare hanky whenever she sat there and would I like a lemon sherbet?

It turned out I would, so that was the end of that.

Once we visited just after the new park keeper started keeping the park. **BAD NANA** was good friends with the old park keeper, Frank, but he had to move to the seaside to be nearer his grandchildren.

Jack pointed out that **BAD NANA** was really lucky as she didn't have to move because she nearly always had her grandchildren with her almost all the time. **BAD NANA** said "*Hmmmmmm*," in a funny way, which I think meant she feels very lucky to have me almost ALL the time but would rather have Jack almost NONE of the time.

DO NOT LAUGH

DO NOT EAT LOLLIES

DO NOT HAVE FUN

DO NOT LITTE

Anyway, we were all super **excited** as we thought the new park keeper might make some **really** good changes to the park . . . like rollercoasters, ice-cream vans and *even* a swimming pool.

It turned out he *had* made **billions** of changes, but NONE of them was a **good** one. Each change was a new **RULE** and he had put them on **signs** all over the place.

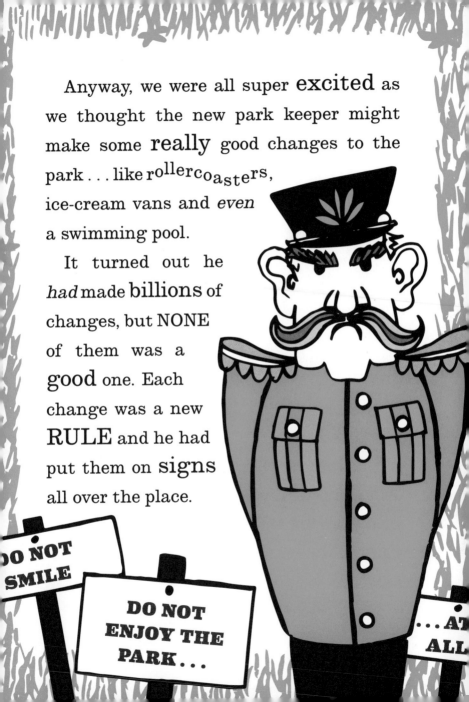

DO NOT SMILE

DO NOT ENJOY THE PARK . . .

. . . AT ALL

There were so many NEW RULES that it made you feel fidgety because you would probably **accidentally** break a rule and then WHO knows what would happen.

DO NOT
ENJOY
YOURSELF

DO NO
PLA
GAM

Everyone in the park seemed really **miserable**, which I don't think is the point of a park at all. I felt practically certain that this would give **BAD NANA** the pip, because if there is **one** thing **BAD NANA** is NOT keen on, it's silly, fun-stopping RULES.

DO NOT
MIME

BAD NANA likes nearly everyone to have fun – that's one of my **favourite** things about her. I could see her getting crosser as she looked about at everyone being all **miserable**, and in such a lovely park too.

DO NOT FEED THE BIRDS

DO NOT DO TWIRLING

Then **BAD NANA** popped in a lemon sherbet, sat on her/*Bill's* bench and had a think. This made me **excited** and **nervous** all at once.

...OR WEAR HATS

DO NOT HAVE PICNICS

As soon as **BAD NANA** had crunched the last of her lemon sherbet, she sprang into ACTION. Well, maybe it was more of a shuffle, but she **definitely** meant business!

After a jolly good rummage in her **humongous** handbag, she told me and Jack to keep our eyes out for the SCARY park keeper while she set about cheering the place up a bit.

I had no idea what this meant and wasn't at all sure how **BAD NANA'S** lippy was going to help. But I DID know that it had given me a funny wriggly feeling in my tummy and it was NOT an entirely good feeling.

It turns out my tummy was spot on as **BAD NANA'S** "cheering the place up a bit" actually meant crossing out all the "NOT"s on the park signs.

Jack and I got quite a bit **nervous** keeping our eyes out and we were both rather relieved when **BAD NANA** had finished.

BAD NANA was especially pleased with her work and felt all the new park signs were "much more encouraging and generally positive". Everyone else seemed to think so too and got back to having lots of fun surprisingly quickly. The park really was very **cheered up** indeed.

We stopped for a bit of a **breather** after all our **rule breaking**/keeping our eyes out, which I was **very** pleased about as I find being a bit **naughty** quite **exhausting**. I have NO idea how **BAD NANA** manages so much **mischief** at her age.

DO NOT ENJOY YOURSELF

DO NOT FEED THE BIRDS

Our **celebrations** didn't last long, though, as apparently the park keeper did NOT want the park **cheered up** AT ALL. In fact, any sort of cheeriness or fun quite clearly made him very CROSS indeed. He was **so CROSS** even his **eyes** seemed to CROSS. I honestly think I saw **smoke** coming out of his **ears**.

He SHOUTED at everyone having fun in the fountain, he BOOMED at all the people enjoying the grass, he YELLED at everyone getting along with the ducks and he SCREAMED at an old lady who was just sniffing a rose.

All the fun **stopped** super-double-quick-fast, which I thought was a real **shame**. I am sure Jack would have thought so too, if he had a **brain**. BAD NANA'S pip came back and she started making rather LOUD grumpy, **humphy** noises until she popped in another lemon sherbet for a think.

The park keeper was stomping about the place,

checking that there was no one still having ANY sort of fun at all and was stomping up the path towards us, with his chest all puffed out like a pigeon in uniform. Just before he got to the bench I heard the crunch of a lemon sherbet and a quiet little cackle from BAD NANA, then I saw a lemon sherbet wrapper float to the ground. It LANDED on the path in front of us.

I was completely SHOCKED as one of **BAD NANA'S** TOP TEN Things of Importance (they are NOT rules – more like firm suggestions) is DON'T DROP LITTER.

But she had just gone and dropped actual litter AND in front of a furious pigeony park keeper. He stomped to a HALT just before the littering sweet wrapper, and his eyes NARROWED as he glared at it and then back at **BAD NANA** and then back at the wrapper. It was extremely tense – SO tense Jack and I might have accidentally held hands. It honestly felt like the whole park was holding its breath. I had no idea how **BAD NANA** was going to wriggle out of this one . . .

BAD NANA looked up and I could see she was giving the park keeper THE BIG EYES and the wiggly OLD-LADY smile. I have seen her use these before in particularly tricky situations. They only properly work when people don't actually know what she is really like. She then leant forward as if she was really trying to pick up the wrapper and made a little noise I have never heard her make before. Like a "fumphfff" or a "finffphfff" or something.

By now all eyes were on the park keeper and he knew it. He couldn't make this little old lady, who seemed to be sort of stuck

on a park bench, pick up
her sweet wrapper, not with
EVERYONE watching and not with
her looking so sweet and everything,
could he? In a way that somehow made it
crystal clear he did not really want to,
the park keeper bent down to
pick the wrapper up . . .

. . . and quick as a flash **BAD NANA** ducked
behind her **massive** handbag and made
the LOUDEST, SQUELCHIEST,
longest,
FARTIEST
raspberry noise.
Ever.

hhhhhhhhhhhhhhhhhhhhhhhhhhhhh

The park keeper straightened up super-duper fast and his face immediately went BRIGHT red. He started flapping about all over the place and saying over and over, "It WASN'T me – it was the OLD LADY!"

But BAD NANA was very busy looking extremely sweet and a bit vague so no one believed him for a second. Or maybe they just didn't want to believe him on account of him being such a fun-stopping stinker all day. So the whole park was now laughing and laughing and that seemed to make the park keeper **redder** and REDDER and I thought he was actually going to go POP. But he didn't. Instead he did a funny little bunny hop – I don't know why – and then RAN all the way to his shed, shut the door and stayed there for the rest of the afternoon.

So we all got to **enjoy** the park again
and **everyone** left it as they had found
it and very definitely put **all** their
rubbish in the **bin** . . .

BAD NANA saw to that!

WINNER WINNER

THE CAT'S PYJAMAS

DO NOT TOUCH

FUNNY BADGE

Jeanie

HIGH 5

THE LOCAL HISTORY MUSEUM
★ ADMIT 1 ★
BRINGING HISTORY TO LIFE

To Jeanie
Thank you!
love
:) Lydia
x x x

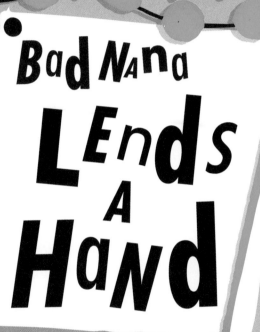

Bad NaNa LEnds A HaNd

BAD Nana

♥

LOL

TOO COOL FOR SKOOL

J

The whole thing started when **BAD NANA** let down the tyres on Mr Pinnock's mobility scooter and everyone agreed she had gone TOO FAR. It didn't matter that Mr Pinnock had been rude to **BAD NANA'S** best friend, Cynth, in the queue at the post office – it was NO EXCUSE!

The next morning, while having a cuppa with Cynth, **BAD NANA** decided she was done with mischief and she would turn over a new leaf. Cynth and I rolled our eyes at each other – we'd heard it all before. But what we hadn't heard before was that this new leaf meant **BAD NANA** would be volunteering to do "good things for others". Well, this was a completely new leaf altogether. I was confused.

I stopped being confused and started being a bit **fed up** when **BAD NANA** told me her first "good thing for others" involved her helping with the reading at MY school.

I have **enough trouble** with Georgina Farquar-Haha sneaking about the place waiting for me to do something **enormously** embarrassing or just a bit **silly** and then **teasing** me about it FOREVER. Sometimes I don't even know I've done anything out of the ordinary, but Georgina **does** and then she makes **sure** everyone else does too. So having **BAD NANA** around at school the whole time was sure to result in me getting a horrible **new** nickname. And I was just getting comfortable with ODD SOCKS JEANIE. I know, it's a **ridiculous** nickname. Even **more** ridiculous when you consider

my socks
weren't even **odd** –
one had just fallen down.

So I felt **ginormously** better when it turned out that **BAD NANA** was "doing good" in Jack's class and helping with reading on Tuesdays and Thursdays.

Once everyone had got the hang of lowering **BAD NANA** into the tiny chairs outside Cherry Class, she really seemed to be doing a very **excellent** job of being READING HELPER. It was all going **really** well and **BAD NANA** was doing lots of "good things", helping Jack and his class read **better**. They all seemed to really enjoy reading with **BAD NANA** and their **vocabulary** was GROWING in all kinds of NEW and interesting ways.

Things only got into a bit of a pickle when Jack's best friend, Ollie, came back from his turn reading with **BAD NANA** and told the class he was a "PROPER DIAMOND GEEZER"* and then asked Miss Peabody what it meant. This made Miss Peabody go a greenish-type colour and rush out of the room to the reading corner.

It turned out that **BAD NANA** had been getting Cherry Class to read her library books, and she had just started a particularly good TRUE-CRIME thriller, which Ollie had been reading. Miss Peabody tried to explain that this was NOT entirely appropriate and **BAD NANA** said she didn't see why as they were much more exciting than the **Hop and Fluff** books and they had lots of new words for the children to learn and that she was saving a fortune on library fines and as they were all based on real-life events it was a bit like history too! But Miss Peabody was quite sure about NOT wanting five-year-olds to read true-crime stories so **BAD NANA** STOPPED being Cherry Class's Reading Helper.

Jack was quite sad about this, but I was completely relieved as I found having **BAD NANA** in school on not only Tuesdays but Thursdays as well was far too nerve-racking.

* "DIAMOND GEEZER" sort of means "good man", but a bit more illegal and dodgier.

I was NOT relieved for long. In fact, quite soon I was totally **unrelieved** as **BAD NANA** happily told me she had volunteered to be a helper on my school trip to *THE LOCAL HISTORY MUSEUM* aka The MOST BORING PLACE EVER. I was so unrelieved I fell over. Actually. For real.

Somehow Miss Peabody hadn't reported **BAD NANA** to the school reception after the reading incident so she was still in the clear to be a school-trip helper. I felt this was very sloppy school security, but as it was too late to do anything I tried to look on the bright side . . . **BAD NANA** could be

LOTS of fun, she always had lemon
sherbets, which were very handy for
coach journeys, and if I was in her group
but Georgina Farquar-Haha wasn't
then it might NOT be a complete, TOTAL,
one hundred per cent disaster.
Maybe.

On the day of the school trip I woke all at sixes and sevens. The butterflies in my tummy had great BIG boots on, and I could *barely* manage my second bowl of Choco Pops.

"Pleeeeeease can **BAD NANA** BEHAVE herself," I said to no one in particular, and tried really, really hard NOT to imagine ALL the absolutely embarrassing things she could do.

Well, even I hadn't bargained for **BAD NANA** trying to get a sing-song going on the bus, but thankfully we were all far too miserable for that.

Normally on school trips we are all giddy with excitement for a whole day out of school. Mr Holmewood usually has to tell us to "calm it DOWN," or we will "PEAK TOO EARLY!" and we never believe him, which is so silly because he is always right.

But today everyone (except for BAD NANA) was pretty quiet on the bus because we had all been here before. Literally. We had all been to *THE LOCAL HISTORY MUSEUM* before, in Year One. So we knew what a completely happy-zapping day of boredom lay ahead.

I would like to point out that I normally really like museums. They are full of INTERESTING facts that are actually INTERESTING, sometimes even head-poppingly INTERESTING. Plus they have levers and pulleys and buttons AND gift shops with fancy pencils. But the main fact you learn at *THE LOCAL HISTORY MUSEUM* is that we do NOT have a lot of history, locally.

I could overlook that, though, if it wasn't for the man who works at *THE LOCAL HISTORY MUSEUM*. He seems to love the museum but hates anyone who visits it, which is very confusing. He is even crosser than the lady in the sweet shop and she is LIVID. This is a mystery to me as how could you even be slightly peeved if you worked in a sweet shop all day long? Mum says it's TOO much sugar.

HALF-MOON GLASSES:
perfect for giving
scary stares over

LIVID EYEBROWS

SUPER BAT HEARING

MAD LASER EYES

Well, it's NOT a smiley
MOUTH, is it?

FURIOUS FLARED NOSTRILS:
the bigger they are the more
furious he is. I know.

CROSS
HUNCHED-UP
SHOULDERS

POINTY
ANGRY
ELBOWS

POCKET FULL
OF LOZENGES:
so all his angry shouting
doesn't give him
a sore throat

IMPATIENT
TAPPY FOOT:
for making you
more nervous

CARDIGAN FOR
EXTRA WARMTH:
as I suspect he is
made of ice

We arrived at the museum and all flopped off the coach. Mr Holmewood didn't have to say "BE QUIET" once, not even to Emily Bartlett, and she is ALWAYS talking.

Mr Holmewood looked a bit worried. Then **BAD NANA** started tutting and eye rolling all at once. I thought she might be having one of her "funny turns" and reached for her bag to get her an emergency lemon sherbet. But as she

THE LOCAL HISTORY MUSEUM
Bringing Local History to Life

swung the bag away and jabbed her bony finger at the museum sign I realised she was NOT having a turn at all but was in actual fact NOT AT ALL HAPPY.

It turns out BAD NANA thought we were visiting the LOCAL **MYSTERY** MUSEUM, which doesn't even exist as far as I know. Anyway BAD NANA LOVES a mystery. Her favourite programme is COSY VILLAGE MURDERS and we are always on the lookout for something SUSPICIOUS. So you can imagine how completely disappointed she was, especially with *THE LOCAL HISTORY MUSEUM* not only being the most boring museum EVER, but having nothing mysterious about it AT ALL. It was a double blow and BAD NANA did not look like she was taking it at all well.

Mr Holmewood put us all into groups and mine was mainly brilliant – it had Marcy AND Wilf in it. Sukey was in another group but she was with her mum and Penny Heard so she didn't really mind. Susie Stubbs and Clare Coleman were in our group and they are sort of friends with Georgia but also sort of NOT (I think they are mainly scared of her and I don't think that is really a good thing for a friendship) so I wasn't too worried about **BAD NANA** doing something double embarrassing.

We also had Lydia in our group. Now, I like Lydia. She is really good at reading and can be quite funny, but she mostly walks on tiptoes so it takes AAAAGES to get anywhere, which is no good for a school trip. I started to feel a bit panicky that we wouldn't get everything done even before Mr Holmewood had handed out the clipboards and worksheets.

We all lined up under the sign:

THE LOCAL HISTORY MUSEUM
Bringing Local History to Life

which was quite funny because it didn't feel very lively at all.

The FURIOUS museum man was already FURIOUS with us for all the things he was sure we were going to do once we got into the museum, e.g. touching things or running about or talking or laughing or breathing or anything that wasn't **STANDING STILL** and **LOOKING/LISTENING**.

We all drooped into the museum like a line of sad zombies. Someone who didn't know us might have thought we were extremely well behaved, but really we were just sad and bored in advance. Lydia tripped up the steps, which I imagine must have been really tricky to navigate on tiptoes, and straight away the FURIOUS museum man barked at her, then gave her such a stinky look that she went all red and her eyes went a bit watery. Wilf and I held her hands hoping it would help. I think it did.

BAD NANA fixed the FURIOUS museum man with her good beady eye and I knew she wasn't going to be taking much more of his nonsense.

The museum tour began and the FURIOUS museum man suddenly started talking like an ANGRY ROBOT, which after about ten minutes sort of makes you sleepy and nervous all at the same time.

After a bit, Freddie made a yipping noise as he had fallen asleep standing up and was having a dream he was a small dog. The FURIOUS museum man shouted

Freddie awake, which, although startling, was actually a good thing as Freddie was dreaming he was being chased by a big dog, hence the yipping.

The FURIOUS museum man then SHOUT-asked Freddie just how was he supposed to *bring history to life* if visitors kept falling asleep? We all considered this for a while and Freddie even started to answer, something about making it more interesting, but Mr Holmewood stepped in and said we could talk about that later. I got the impression it was one of those questions grown-ups ask, but they don't actually want an answer for.

During the next looooooooooooong lecture the FURIOUS museum man shouted at Georgina for sneezing, Tim for coughing, Sally for hiccupping (which is double awful as Sally said she only got the hiccups because the FURIOUS museum man made her SO nervous) and Sukey's mum for fidgeting.

Then he made a HUGE shouty mistake by YELLING at BAD NANA for sucking too loudly on a lemon sherbet and even suggested she had surely had enough lemon sherbets already.

Well, that was it. BAD NANA'S good beady eye NARROWED and she went a very bright shade of purpley red, which I had never seen her go before. I mean I have seen her go pink, I've seen her go reddish, even red, but I have never seen the purpley red and I could only imagine this was **NOT A GOOD THING.**

FINALLY the lecture stopped and we were given **worksheets**. Mr Holmewood looked confused when we all grabbed them happily, that had **never** happened before. Anything was better than listening to the FURIOUS museum man talking about the almost **non-existent** local history in his ANGRY ROBOT voice.

As I took my clipboard from Mr Holmewood, Georgina gave me one of those "I'm watching YOU, **Odd Socks**" looks and I tried to make sure I was being completely **normal** and in no way doing anything that looked **odd** or different or tease-able.

I was concentrating so hard on this that I accidentally walked into a stand with a reproduction vase that the FURIOUS museum man thought might have been a bit like the one they had in the museum a million years ago when it was actually a house.

The vase **wibbled**, and then it **wobbled**, and it **wibbled** a bit **more** and then it **fell** down. The FURIOUS museum man **dived** and tried to **catch** the vase, but he was miles away and actually, it just looked like he fell over all of a sudden. But **Billy** caught it instead as he was right there and an excellent **goalkeeper** on

our school

football

team.

Phew! I thought, but then I thought again as the FURIOUS museum man got up, dusted himself down and then started yelling at me so SUPER-DUPER loudly I couldn't quite make out what he was saying. It all just *blurred* into one long FOGHORN-TYPE noise. But I did get the impression that what he was saying wasn't at all good. I am not sure how long this would have gone on for had **BAD NANA** not inserted herself between me and the FURIOUS museum man and told him in no uncertain terms that "accidents happen", there was "no harm done" and that "THAT was quite enough of that". The FURIOUS museum man gave **BAD NANA** a funny look, like he had just swallowed some super-hot chilli sauce, but **BAD NANA** didn't even blink, and off he stomped.

I felt a little bit **wobbly**, like I had been
in a *WIND TUNNEL* turned to MAX, but
BAD NANA snuck each of us a lemon sherbet,
for medicinal purposes, and we were off.
Everyone was **bobbing** about trying

to be the first group to finish. It turns out Lydia has got quite fast on her tiptoes, what with mainly walking on them and everything, so we were doing really well, until . . .

We were all shuffling past the pretend old bedroom in a sort of SAD conga line. There were fancy ropes that stopped us actually going into the pretend old bedroom, which were quite a bit fancier than the actual bedroom, if I am really honest.

Georgina was right in front of us and telling (boring) the rest of her group about her upcoming dance showcase with Glitter Bugs, the dance group she belongs to. I am not sure it is strictly dancing as it looks more like ELECTRIC SHOCKS and flinging yourself about the place to me.

But I have to say the way they make their hair stay straight up and not move one inch, no matter how much they fling themselves and jump about, is actually very impressive.

Glitter Bugz

Anyway Georgina was explaining a particularly **tricky** part of their DISCO routine and no one knew (cared) what she was on about so, with a hairflick/eye-roll combo that quite clearly said we were all **idiots**, she **demonstrated** the move.

It was really extremely **energetic** and so SUPER FAST I couldn't tell you **exactly** which body part she moved. But what I do know is that the body part hit

Lydia, whose balance was already off, what with her being on tiptoes, so she went *flying* with such DISCO force that the red ropes didn't stop her going into the pretend old bedroom at all. All I heard was a FLUMPHF and a cloud of dust flew up from the bed, and all we could see were Lydia's toes, still pointed, hanging over the end of the pretend old bed.

We all stood super **still**, like musical statues professionals, then Mr Holmewood rushed forward to **rescue** Lydia from the dust, which was settling back down all over her. He needn't have bothered because the FURIOUS man's **bellowing** unsettled the dust all over again. To say he was FURIOUS was like saying I only like egg sandwiches when I actually LOVE egg sandwiches (even if I can only eat them in the safety of my own home now). He was now **definitely** infinity FURIOUS. Even Mr Holmewood looked paler than usual as he stood behind Lydia while the FURIOUS man SHOUTED at her.

But then that could have been the dust.

Lydia had gone all **red** again and her eyes were **watering** too and it was all so super **unfair** because it wasn't even her fault, but the **real** culprit, DISCO-**dancing** Georgina, had shimmied away when the yelling started.

When I looked at **BAD NANA** I could see she was that purpley-red colour again and I could hardly even see her good beady eye it was so narrowed.

Lunchtime **should** have been **fun**, what with **comparing** packed lunches, **swapping** snacks and **eating** on the grass, but it WASN'T. Lydia's eyes were still watery and this wasn't helped by Georgina making **snoring** noises and asking her if it was bedtime as she slunk by with her group.

I knew Georgina was a total **meanie**

but I didn't expect her to cause a **complete catastrophe**, not EVEN own up and then tease the person she'd inflicted the complete catastrophe upon. This was a new low, **even** for her.

We **slowly** and **bravely** ate our sandwiches, crisps, biscuits and healthy fruit snacks as **BAD NANA** pointed out we would need our strength for the rest of the visit. We all nodded sadly.

After lunch, we gathered in the Great Hall (it WASN'T great but it was a hall) and the FURIOUS museum man yelled at us about how AAAAGES ago some posh people would have dinner in this actual room. Apparently some people even thought an old round king had popped by for a feast and eaten LOADS. That's not EXACTLY how the FURIOUS museum man said it, but that's basically what he meant.

Then he said we had to draw an olden-days feast, just like the one they had

set up in the Great Hall using
some slightly frightening-looking
mannequins, an old wooden
table and some **dusty** papier-
mâché food. I thought it looked
a bit like Christmas
at Aunty Sandra's
house, minus the
paper hats.

As we all sat down in total silence and started to draw, the FURIOUS museum man marched about and said absolutely NOTHING nice about anyone's pictures.

Then he stopped by Lydia, whose eyes had only just stopped watering, and he looked at her picture. Then, for the first time all day, he smiled. I nearly fell straight over – maybe he wasn't completely FURIOUS after all, maybe he was actually slightly NOT horrible, maybe . . .

But then his smile turned into a creepy sneer and the creepy sneer turned into a NASTY laugh and then the FURIOUS museum man was nastily laughing and creepily sneering and even EVILLY pointing at poor Lydia's drawing. If I am going to be one hundred per cent totally honest, drawing isn't Lydia's best skill, but you can't be good at everything and she is REALLY good at reading and, anyway, I thought it looked a lot like an olden-times feast, sort of.

Georgina, who is never one to miss out on a bit of picking-on-innocent-people-just-minding-their-own-business, h^opped over and looked at Lydia's drawing and started NASTILY laughing too, which was double annoying as she was the one who had got Lydia into trouble earlier.

Then everyone else started to laugh because if Georgina is laughing and she's not laughing at you then you'd better join in or else.

With all the NASTY laughing and creepy sneering and EVIL pointing, it wasn't at all surprising that Lydia's eyes started to water and water and she went all pink and looked very wobbly, even though she was sitting down and not even on tiptoes.

I looked around for BAD NANA because I knew she wouldn't be having any of this nonsense, but as I turned round all I could see was her back disappearing behind a curtain. WHAT? Where was she hobbling off to when her group needed her? It was not at all like BAD NANA to shy away from trouble.

I was completely confused and all the LOUD laughing wasn't helping. It was all so unfair and I just couldn't let Lydia and her tiptoes down. Then I realised I had to do something because it really didn't look like anyone else was going to.

I stood up, and I wibbled around a bit because I wasn't **really** sure what I was going to do next and my tummy was doing all kinds of gymnastics and I started to say "STOP!" but it sounded more like a "Squwark!" because my throat was all tight and I looked at Wilf and he was mouthing "WHAT ARE YOU DOING?" at me and I mouthed back "I DON'T KNOW!" while shrugging my shoulders for extra emphasis, and then I looked at Lydia with her pink and watery face and I tried again . . .

"STOP IT!" I shouted. This time my throat let the actual words out and everyone but the FURIOUS museum man STOPPED. I think they were all a bit surprised because I am not really the shouting type. Then I shouted again "STOP IT, please." (Because manners are still important even if you are talking to a completely mean FURIOUS museum man.) "YOU are just being horrible and mean and NASTY and horrible and . . ."

By this point I realised that he had stopped laughing and the smiley sneer had been replaced by a FURIOUS face, which funnily enough looked almost exactly the SAME as one of the stone gargoyles he had been wiffling on about earlier.

I was a bit stuck then because my brain decided to stop thinking entirely and I just stood there like a total twit with my mouth hanging open and no idea what to do next. This was quite a worry as I could feel the FURIOUS museum man was about to say something and I felt, very strongly, that what he was going to say was NOT going to work out too well for me.

SPOT THE DIFFERENCE...

"YOUNG LADY . . ."

he boomed, and although this was a promising start, and not totally insulting, I was very sure it was going to get worse . . .

"WHEN YOU ARE IN MY MUSEUM, ***THE LOCAL HISTORY MUSEUM*** *Bringing Local History to Life*, I THINK YOU WILL FIND THAT I CAN DO JUST ABOUT WHATEVER I PLEASE AND FURTHERMORE . . ."

Well, we never did get any further or hear any more because just then a dusty papier-mâché chicken drumstick hit the FURIOUS museum man on the side of his head. Then a dusty papier-mâché apple came flying over and "missed" him and got Georgina on the forehead. We all turned round to see **where** these things were coming from and saw that history had **actually** really **truly** come to life.

AMAZINGLY the round king in the display was chuckling away merrily and **hurling** all kinds of papier-mâché food about, but mainly in the direction of the FURIOUS museum man, who was now **more FURIOUS** than ever. But hardly anyone really **noticed** as they were all **dancing** around in front of the display, enjoying *Local History Being Brought To Life* by the round, chuckling king.

Everyone started asking the round king lots of **questions** because it's not very often you can quiz a sixteenth-century king, **chuckling** or not. I wanted to ask the round king why all of a sudden he was wearing **ginormous** glasses and earrings that gave him a little bit of **twinkle**, but I decided not to as everyone was enjoying themselves **too** much.

I am not sure all the answers the round king gave were **strictly** correct, and Mr Holmewood had to help him out with a few, but all in all I think **everyone** got **something** out of it. Even the FURIOUS museum man, because he got **THE SULKS**.

Big time.

When it was time to go and we were all lining up, the SULKY museum man announced **very** loudly that our school would no longer be welcome at *THE LOCAL HISTORY MUSEUM – No Longer Bringing History to Life* because we **clearly** didn't **appreciate** our local history and I thought that was odd because after the round king came to life it seemed like **absolutely** everyone in my class appreciated history quite a LOT (except for Brian Hargreaves, but then he is only interested in OUTER SPACE and wine gums). I thought I saw Mr Holmewood do a little **smile** when he heard this and maybe **high-five** the coach driver, but I might have been mistaken. (I WASN'T.)

WAY OUT
(and don't come back)

BAD NANA came tottering up to the coach at quite a *PACE* for her. She was all out of breath and looked rather warm, which might have had something to do with the red beard she was sporting. Wilf and Lydia and Susie and Clare all ran up to her, yelping about everything that had just happened and asking where she was and wasn't it a shame she missed all the fun? Very hilariously, they didn't seem to notice the beard at all, which I thought spoke very poorly of their image of **BAD NANA**. We were all in total fits about the chuckling round king and the *flying* papier-mâché food and Georgina's apple in the face and the FURIOUS museum man's sulks.

On the bus on the way home, after I had signalled to **BAD NANA** to remove her beard, I thought about all the future classes who would no longer have to visit *THE LOCAL HISTORY MUSEUM – Definitely Not Bringing History to Life*, and how I had played a small part in that, and how **BAD NANA** had played a big part in that, and how Georgina was now calling me Jeanie Parrot Pants on account of my SQUAWK. Which just goes to show three things . . .

1. Georgina will give me super-rubbish nicknames no matter what I do so I really can't be worrying about all that. Well, not too much anyway.

And 2. There is a small chance that I will be regarded as a tiny bit of a hero by future pupils at my school who will not have to visit the most boring and FURIOUS museum in the world, ever. Maybe there would even be a plaque in my honour.

And 3. That while BAD NANA may have been a little bit naughty and maybe even a tiny bit embarrassing, she is mainly brilliant.